Veterinarian

Jeff Barger

Rourke™

ROURKE'S
SCHOOL to HOME
CONNECTIONS
BEFORE AND DURING READING ACTIVITIES

Before Reading: *Building Background Knowledge and Vocabulary*

Building background knowledge can help children process new information and build upon what they already know. Before reading a book, it is important to tap into what children already know about the topic. This will help them develop their vocabulary and increase their reading comprehension.

Questions and Activities to Build Background Knowledge:

1. Look at the front cover of the book and read the title. What do you think this book will be about?
2. What do you already know about this topic?
3. Take a book walk and skim the pages. Look at the table of contents, photographs, captions, and bold words. Did these text features give you any information or predictions about what you will read in this book?

Vocabulary: *Vocabulary Is Key to Reading Comprehension*

Use the following directions to prompt a conversation about each word.

- Read the vocabulary words.
- What comes to mind when you see each word?
- What do you think each word means?

Vocabulary Words:

- *medicine*
- *microscope*
- *stethoscopes*
- *x-rays*

During Reading: *Reading for Meaning and Understanding*

To achieve deep comprehension of a book, children are encouraged to use close reading strategies. During reading, it is important to have children stop and make connections. These connections result in deeper analysis and understanding of a book.

Close Reading a Text

During reading, have children stop and talk about the following:

- Any confusing parts
- Any unknown words
- Text to text, text to self, text to world connections
- The main idea in each chapter or heading

Encourage children to use context clues to determine the meaning of any unknown words. These strategies will help children learn to analyze the text more thoroughly as they read.

When you are finished reading this book, turn to the next-to-last page for an **After Reading Activity**.

Table of Contents

Community Helpers

Community helpers are all around us. They make our lives better.

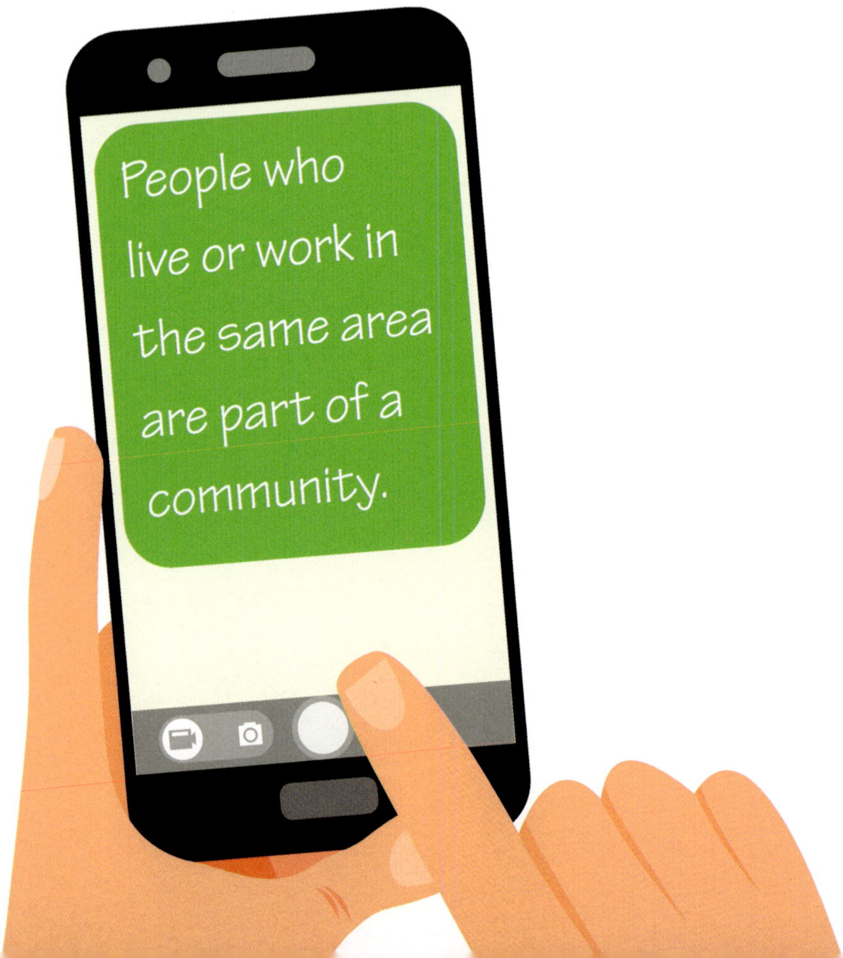

Your pet is sick.

A veterinarian can help.

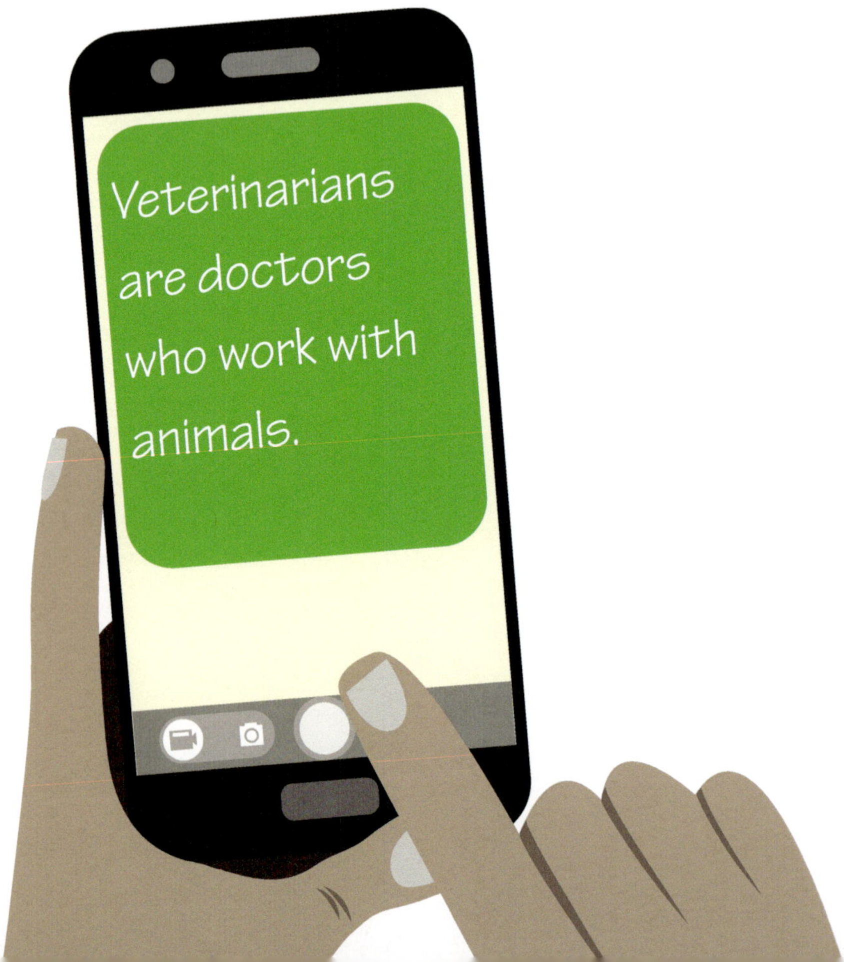

A Visit to the Vet

The vet sees your pet.

They ask questions.

The vet uses a tool.

It helps them listen to your pet's breathing.

Blood is taken. The vet will test it.

X-rays may also be used.

Your pet must sit quietly.

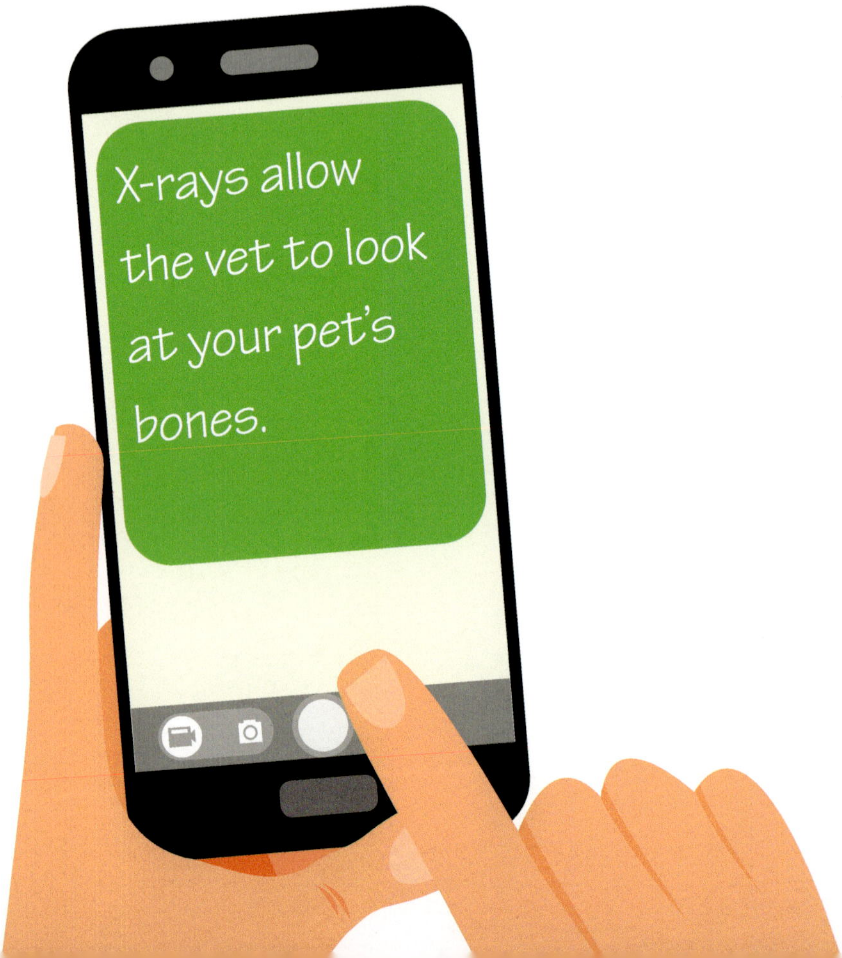

The vet sees the problem.

They give **medicine** to help.

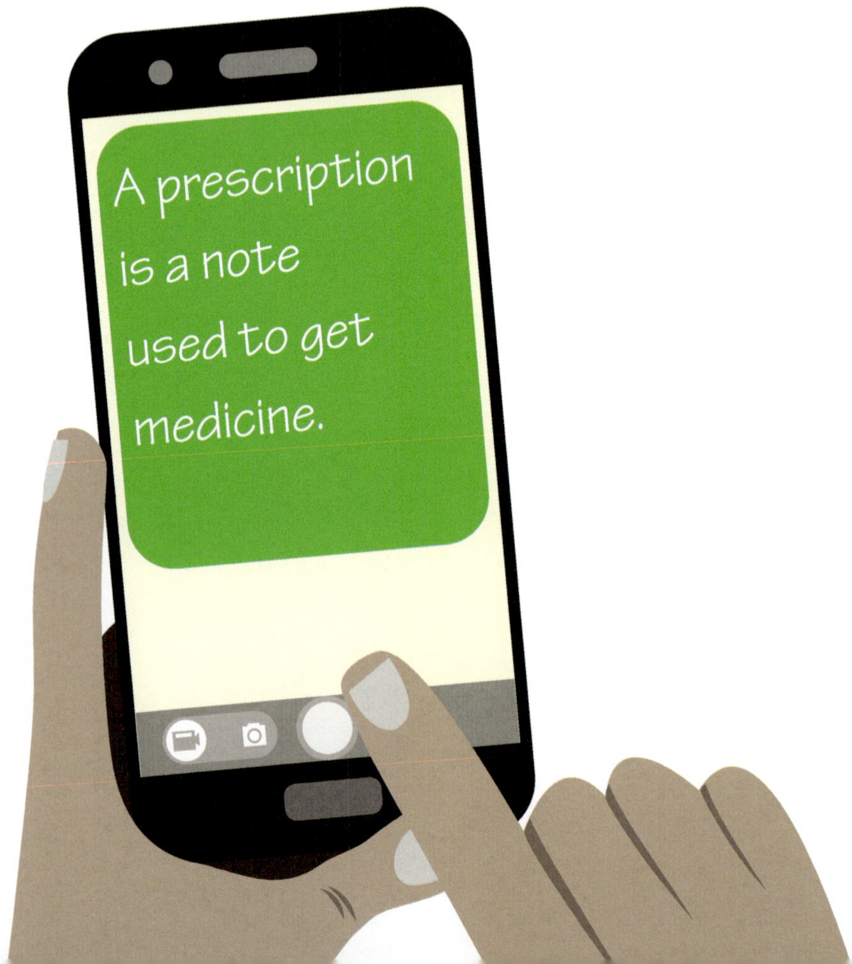

Large Animals Need Care

Some vets go to farms.

They care for large animals.

Sick animals need care.

A vet is their doctor.

Activity

Keeping Pets Healthy

Supplies

- paper
- crayons
- markers
- pencil

Directions

1. Choose a pet. Think about someone who is a new owner of this pet. What would the owner need to know to take good care of the pet? If you need to, do some research.
2. Write and draw a poster that gives three ideas you would share with the new pet owner.

Photo Glossary

medicine (MED-i-sin): A drug that is used to treat an illness.

microscope (MYE-kruh-skope): A tool that makes very small things look larger so that they can be seen and studied.

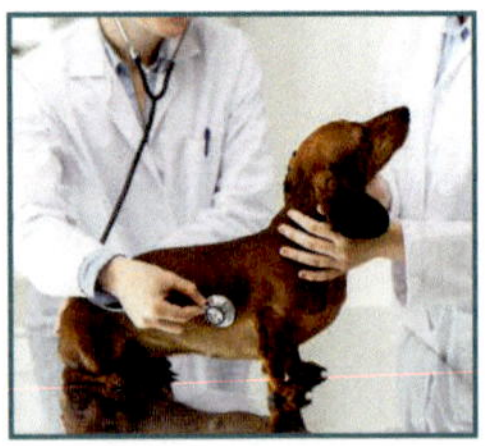

stethoscopes (STETH-uh-skopes): Tools used by doctors and nurses to listen to the sounds from a patient's heart, lungs, and other parts of the body.

x-rays (EKS-rays): Pictures of the inside of a patient's body.

Index

After Reading Activity

Pretend that you are a veterinarian. Think of three things you might say to an animal that you were treating or to its owner.

About the Author

Jeff Barger is an author, blogger, and literacy specialist. He lives in North Carolina. Jeff behaves at the vet's office, but they don't give him any treats.

www.rourkebooks.com

Edited by: Kim Thompson
Cover and interior design by: Kathy Walsh

Photo Credits: Cover, title page, p.20: ©gilaxia; p.5: ©Rawpixel.com; p.7, 9: ©Mordolff; p.11, 22: ©dolgachov; p.13, 22: ©bweber53; p.15, 22: ©fofoedu; p.17, 22: ©Vasyl Dolmatov; p.19: ©Wavebreakermedia

Library of Congress PCN Data

Veterinarian / Jeff Barger
(Community Helpers)
ISBN 978-1-73161-425-4 (hard cover)(alk. paper)
ISBN 978-1-73161-220-5 (soft cover)
ISBN 978-1-73161-530-5 (e-Book)
ISBN 978-1-73161-635-7 (ePub)
Library of Congress Control Number: 2019932042

Rourke Educational Media
Printed in the United States of America
01-2972211937